EMILY BRONTË'S

WUTHERING HEIGHTS

A RETELLING BY TANYA LANDMAN

UNION SQUARE & CO.
NEW YORK

UNION
SQUARE
& CO.

NEW YORK

UNION SQUARE & CO. and the distinctive Union Square & Co. logo are trademarks of Sterling Publishing Co., Inc.

Union Square & Co., LLC, is a subsidiary of Sterling Publishing Co., Inc.

First published in Great Britain in 2020 by Barrington Stoke Ltd. First published in the United States and Canada in 2024 by Union Square & Co., LLC.

ISBN 978-1-4549-5483-5

Library of Congress Control Number: 2023942901

For information about custom editions, special sales, and premium purchases, please contact specialsales@unionsquareandco.com.

Printed in China

2 4 6 8 10 9 7 5 3 1

unionsquareandco.com

Union Square & Co.'s EVERYONE CAN BE A READER books are expertly written, thoughtfully designed with dyslexia-friendly fonts and paper tones, and carefully formatted to meet readers where they are with engaging stories that encourage reading success across a wide range of age and interest levels.

For Isaac and Jack: a Joseph-free version

A stranger is lying in my bed. He has helped himself to my books. His pudgy fingers are tracing the words I wrote as a child. Words meant for no one but myself. Words no one else should read.

And now the stranger is speaking aloud the names I scratched into the paint on the window ledge.

Catherine Earnshaw—the girl I was born.

Catherine Linton—the wife I became.

Catherine Heathcliff—who I should have been.

Catherine Heathcliff—who I was in my heart.

Catherine Heathcliff—who I was in my soul.

The stranger pronounces each name in turn, uttering them over and over until the air swarms with Catherines. It's a calling. A summons. He's given me form, brought me into being—a child lost and wandering on the moor for twenty years but now come home.

He sees me, but he will not let me in. He is cruel, this stranger. I grasp his wrist with my small, cold hand and beg most pitifully, but he shows no mercy. The stranger tries to pry my fingers from his arm. When he cannot, he grinds my wrist on the window's broken glass. My blood runs down onto the window ledge, pooling, blotting out my names.

And now Heathcliff is here. Calling me, begging me, "Cathy, do come. Oh, do—once more! Oh, my heart's darling, hear me this time!"

"I am here," I tell him. Because I always have been.

But Heathcliff does not hear me. He does not see. He cannot.

Not yet.

1.

I was always too much of one thing and too little of the other. Too loud. Too rowdy. Too willful. Not meek or mild or gentle enough. Not ladylike. Mother and Father and the maid scolded me constantly, "Why can't you be a good girl, Cathy? Why can't you behave?" The more they asked, the worse I got.

When I was six years old, Father said he was going to Liverpool. Sixty miles there, sixty miles back, and he was walking the whole way. If Father told us the reason for his journey, I can't recall it. He'd be gone three days, he said, and when he returned to Wuthering Heights he'd bring us presents.

When Father asked what we wanted, my brother Hindley said, "A fiddle." Father gave him a smile, for he liked to think of his son as a musician. Then Father looked at me. I saw the hope in his eyes. He wanted me to be like Beauty in *Beauty and the Beast* and ask him for something simple that costs nothing. A kingfisher's feather perhaps, or the shell of a robin's egg, or the first rose of summer plucked from a hedgerow.

I opened my mouth to speak, but before the words came out I saw something else in Father's eyes, something deeper. It was a shadow of desperation, an expectation of disappointment. At that moment I knew I'd never measure up, no matter how hard I tried. It just wasn't in me to be the obedient, devoted daughter my father craved. And I was sick of trying to be her. So I said I wanted a whip with an ivory handle carved in the shape of a tiger's head, inlaid with silver and gold, and with rubies for its eyes. It should be long and supple too so I could beat my pony to shreds when it did not gallop fast enough.

*

I suffered two full days of Mother's nagging and the maid's scolding while Father was gone. My brother, Hindley, was allowed to do whatever he pleased and to go wherever he wanted, for boys will be boys. But I had to be sweet-natured and obedient and help around the house.

On the morning of the third day I slipped away from Mother's grasp, running onto the moor, my skirts raised high, as barefoot as a beggar. I ran until the pain in my side tore at me so hard I could run no more. By then I'd reached the high, rocky cliffs. The day was warm and I lay back on the springy turf and shut my eyes. I could feel the earth pulsing beneath my back. I could hear the throbbing of its life force as if I were a baby in my mother's belly, listening to her heart beat. I felt a tug at my chest, something pulling at me, and then I was breaking free . . . I rose up out of myself into the spring air, flying with the shorebirds into the blue sky, carried on the wind toward the billowing clouds. I looked down and could see my body far below me, scrunched up like a piece of wastepaper. And being good or bad didn't matter anymore. I was tumbling, spinning, whirling, purely and fully myself, while at the same time lost in Nature.

When I snapped back to my body on the ground, I could barely breathe. My ribs seemed as tight as a brutally laced corset. My body held me as securely as if it were a prison.

2.

Father was expected home in the afternoon. As the light faded, Hindley and I ran down to the gate once, twice, three times, but there was no sign of him. Mother put off supper for one hour, then two. Bedtime came and went and we still waited. It was close to midnight when the door latch was raised and in Father came looking as pale as death and so weary he could barely set one foot in front of the other. He staggered under the weight of a bundle he carried in his arms and collapsed into a chair, groaning. It was only after Father had drunk a little of the brandy Mother held to his lips that he managed to speak.

Father told me and Hindley that we must wait for our presents: first, he had one for Mother. "It's a gift from God, I believe," he said. "Though he's dark as the night."

Carefully, Father unwrapped his bundle. Inside was a child, a boy maybe a year older than me. His arms and legs were stick-thin, his cheeks hollowed, his eyes too big for his head. The boy stank to high heaven. I remember thinking that I was no Beauty, but Father had brought home the Beast.

Mother was horrified, her mouth hanging open. There was a long silence, broken only by the ticking of the clock and the crackle of the fire. And then Mother erupted at Father. "Are you serious? Haven't we got our own children to feed and clothe? What are you thinking, bringing home a filthy beggar boy?"

Father said he'd found the child wandering alone in the street. No one knew who he was or where he had come from. He could hardly leave the boy to starve, Father said. Saving him was his Christian duty.

Christian.

Duty.

They were two words Mother couldn't argue with. She rumbled on at Father a while longer, but her temper finally rolled away like a passing thunderstorm. Father told the maid, Nelly, to take care of the child, to wash him and give him clean clothes. When that was done, Father said, the boy could sleep in the room I shared with Hindley and Nelly.

And maybe the boy would have done so, and maybe things would have turned out fine. But before Nelly led the boy away, Hindley started poking around in Father's coat pockets. He pulled out the fiddle he'd asked for, but it was in pieces, having been accidentally crushed on the journey. Despite being a strapping boy more than twice my age, my brother began to scream like a baby. No one told him to hush himself or be good. It so enraged me that when Father said my whip had gotten lost on the moor, I spat in the face of the beggar child. It had to be his fault.

There was a moment's hush. A moment's perfect stillness. I looked into the boy's crow-black eyes. We both looked so deep that somehow—don't ask me how—our souls seemed to tumble headlong into each other. I was speechless. My heart beat so hard against my ribs I feared they might break.

Then Father hit me. "Mind your manners," he said, and gave me a great slap to the side of my head that sent blood rushing to my ears. I did not cry, and for that I was called cold and unnatural.

The rest of that evening is something of a blur now. Father and Mother must have gone to bed, leaving Nelly in charge. The boy got a violent washing from her, for Nelly liked the intruder as little as Hindley did. She did not care how icy was the water or how hard the scrubbing brush. Nelly fetched out an old nightshirt of my brother's, a garment far too big for the boy. After that, Hindley would not allow him into the room we shared. Nelly bolted the door against the boy and he spent that first night curled on the landing outside Father's room like a dog.

But I remember one thing clearly. I didn't object to Nelly's treatment—not because I agreed with it but because I was too shocked, too stunned to say or do anything. Something strange had happened to me in that moment after I'd spat in his face and before Father had hit me. Something I had no words to describe.

*

In the morning, Father tripped over the boy on the landing. He soon discovered how his foundling child had been treated by Nelly and was so enraged he sent the maid packing. But her banishment didn't last more than a week, for it was hard to get servants to come to a house as remote as ours and Mother couldn't manage without her. By the time Nelly returned, the beggar boy had been named Heathcliff, and he and I were as close as needle and thread. My soul was not confined in my body anymore—it had spilled across to his. I was Heathcliff. He was me. And the two of us together were bigger than the sky and freer than the wind.

3.

Two years passed. The affinity Heathcliff and I had would have been strong under any circumstances, but the hatred we shared toward my brother made our bond as solid as granite.

From the very outset, Hindley could not forgive Heathcliff's existence or Father's fondness for the "bastard brat," as Hindley called him. My brother might have managed things better had he been cunning or clever. Hindley could have bided his time. He could have smiled at Heathcliff and pretended to be friends while quietly undermining him. But Hindley was a sledgehammer of a boy who swung blindly at whatever angered him and ended up knocking out only himself.

To begin with, Hindley had allies in his war against Heathcliff. Mother turned a blind eye to Hindley's bullying. Nelly would pinch and prod and punish Heathcliff for invented crimes whenever she got the chance. Father was busy with the running of the farm, but if he noticed any instances of cruelty—and there were many—he would take Heathcliff's side every time. Mother would defend Hindley, so hour after hour, day after day, week after week Wuthering Heights was in uproar.

But then Mother died. I can't say I grieved for her. She'd scolded and screamed at me all the days of my life—her absence was a relief. But Hindley was distraught. He'd lost his most powerful ally. And not long after Mother was laid in the ground, Nelly's attitude to Heathcliff softened. I don't know what it was that caused her to desert Hindley, but he was left to rant and rave against his adopted brother all alone. Hindley gave us no peace and Father despaired of him. At last, Hindley was sent away to college to be turned into a gentleman. Heathcliff and I were left to run free.

Oh, I know what folk said. I heard the whispers when we were in church. The Lintons of Thrushcross Grange muttered to the Braithwaites from Gimmerton behind upraised hands that Heathcliff and I were an unruly, wicked, willful pair. Hadn't the sexton seen us playing in the churchyard after dark, dancing between the graves? Hadn't the gamekeeper seen us running half naked over the moors? Weren't we a disgrace to God and man?

Perhaps we were. But what did we care what the gossips said? In our eyes, only Heathcliff and I were real beings: other people were just shadows. Nelly tried to tame us and Father pleaded for us to behave in a proper fashion, but we would not, could not be bound by them. We were wild, I admit that. We'd lie on our backs, staring at the sky, letting our spirits soar on the wings of the birds above. We'd strip naked and bathe in the icy waters of the creek. We'd shriek with delight running downhill, feeling we were about to take flight. And we'd laugh at something, nothing, anything. We'd laugh until we were breathless and so weak we could hardly stand. The idea of right and wrong, of good and evil, did not apply to us any more than they applied to a fox stalking across grass or a hawk riding the wind. Past, future, salvation, damnation meant nothing. There was only the here and now. Heaven for us was being together up on the cliff. Hell was being separated after we'd pushed Father too far and he'd decided to punish us.

4.

For a few years Heathcliff and I lived in paradise and I thought it would last forever. But then came one dreary October evening, when the wind shrieked about the house and set all the windows rattling. That evening, a catastrophe brought everything tumbling down around our ears.

I was twelve years old and Heathcliff around thirteen. We were gathered by the fire: Nelly with her knitting on one side, Father in his chair on the other, me sitting on the floor leaning against Father's knees. Heathcliff lay stretched out, basking in the fire's warmth like a cat, his head in my lap. We'd tired ourselves out that day and I suppose we were oddly quiet, for Father laid a hand on my head and said, "Why can't you always be a good girl, Cathy?"

I laughed and replied, "Why can't you always be a good man, Father?"

Poor thing! Father could no more understand me joking than he could when I was being serious. He winced as if I'd struck him. His look was so upset that I regretted my teasing words. I kissed Father's hand and then began to sing one of his favorite songs in a low voice to soothe him to sleep.

Father's hand slipped from my head as he fell into a doze. For a good half hour or more we sat as quiet as mice. We might all be sitting there still if Nelly hadn't decided it was time for bed.

I stood up to wish Father good night. Putting my arms around his neck, I was about to kiss his cheek. But something stopped me. Sleep and death might look the same, but they are so very different. His skin was still warm, his face hadn't changed. But my father had gone and all that was left in his chair was an empty shell.

"Oh, he's dead, Heathcliff!" I cried. "He's dead!"

I remember weeping that night, weeping bitterly. I thought I'd killed him. I wept and wept and wept. For Father. For myself. For Heathcliff. He and I clung to each other like shipwrecked souls in a storm. We both knew that no good would come of this. None at all.

5.

Hindley came home for Father's funeral and he brought a wife with him: a woman he'd never thought to mention in his letters to Father. How everyone gossiped! The Lintons and the Braithwaites were gaping, their eyes bugging out. Heathcliff and I were all but forgotten in the light of Hindley and his wife.

Hindley was twenty years old by then, his wife two or three years younger. He looked different: he'd grown taller, leaner, more handsome. But his temperament was as ugly as it had ever been. Hindley was a man now, the master of Wuthering Heights, and his bride was its mistress, though she couldn't have been more empty-headed, prattling, and useless. Her name was Frances and she was a dainty, delicate thing, pretty enough and with sparkling eyes. She fussed over me to begin with, calling me "sister," saying we'd be such fine friends, trying to buy my affection with gifts of ribbons and the like.

Frances should have saved her breath and her gifts. I hated every fiber of her being. She'd looked down her nose at Heathcliff the moment she'd stepped into the house. That alone had made me furious. But then she'd called Heathcliff dirty and shuddered as if he were something disgusting and repellent.

Before Father was even cold in his grave, Hindley had demoted Heathcliff from family member to servant. Heathcliff was ordered about, Hindley's words falling like clods of earth on a coffin lid. Heathcliff was no longer to dine with us at the table but to keep to the back kitchen with Nelly and the farmhands. Heathcliff was to receive no more lessons alongside me but to work for his keep.

It was harsh and cruel and it went against Father's wishes, but in truth it came as no great surprise to Heathcliff and me. To begin with, we carried on much as before. Heathcliff was banished out of doors. So what? We preferred the open air in any case. I joined Heathcliff in the fields if there was work that needed doing, and if not we'd run off across the moors. I attended my lessons as usual, and in the evenings I passed on everything I'd learned to Heathcliff.

Hindley liked to chastise us. He'd order Heathcliff to be flogged, and if he could find no one to carry out the beating, he'd do it himself. Hindley would lock me in my room and deprive me of my dinner. But such things had no power to touch us. The more tyrannical Hindley grew, the more reckless we became. Heathcliff and I were engaged in a battle with Hindley and having our old enemy back brought us closer than ever. We plotted against my brother. We would pay him back one day, we solemnly swore. We noted every blow, every harsh word, every withheld meal, and we would repay it and then some when the time came. We would have our revenge one day. We would see Hindley in the ground and send his wife packing, and then the two of us would dance together on his grave.

*

Our plans for the future—such as they were—changed one Sunday. I'd ridden to church as usual with Hindley and Frances and been preached at for an hour or more about Hell and damnation. We'd ridden back and now the afternoon stretched out ahead of us, long and tedious. We sat in the parlor, Frances perched on her husband's knee talking foolish nonsense, hogging all the heat from the fire, while I sat shivering in a corner.

I did something wrong, though I don't know what: sneezed, maybe, or breathed too loudly in their presence. Whatever it was, I was sent out of the room in punishment, ordered to sit in the kitchen, read my bible, and pray. But if I was out of the room and out of Hindley's sight, I might as well be out of the house too, I thought. I lifted the latch and slipped out in search of Heathcliff.

We ran faster and farther than we'd ever gone that day. I'd lost my shoes in the bog and the light was beginning to fade. But instead of turning for home we turned our backs to Wuthering Heights and looked in the other direction.

"Suppose we keep running?" I said. "Suppose we don't go back at all?"

Heathcliff laughed. "How will we live?" he asked.

I shrugged. "As birds do."

Heathcliff's face became pinched and he seemed to fall into some dark, desolate place where I could not reach him. He was silent for a long time and then he said, "I could not stand to see you go hungry, Cathy."

I opened my mouth to say I'd survive—I was always being sent to bed without my supper. But the words dried on my lips when I looked at him. The hunger Heathcliff was talking about went deeper than one withheld meal.

Darkness had gathered itself around us like a cape. Down in the valley we saw a light from Thrushcross Grange. We'd never set foot over the threshold, but we both knew it was where the Lintons lived—we never spoke but saw them in church every week. Mr. Linton was a government official, an upstanding citizen. His wife was a pillar of the church. They were a respectable family: two God-fearing parents and two polite, well-behaved children. Their son, Edgar, was perhaps two years older than Heathcliff. Their daughter, Isabella, was a year younger than me. I'd never had any interest in them whatsoever.

But now I was overcome with curiosity. I knew nothing of the world beyond Wuthering Heights. How did other people get by? How did they live? What did they do on an evening?

Heathcliff read my thoughts.

"Let's take a look," he said.

6.

We had to push past a hedge and grope our way across a vast garden before we got to the house. The light flooded out from the drawing room because the curtains were only half closed. We peered in, and oh! What a sight met our eyes.

Wuthering Heights was a farmhouse, with walls built thick to keep out the howling wind and blizzards that came off the moor, its ceilings low and windows narrow. Thrushcross Grange was like something out of a fairy tale. Everything was crimson and white and gold, including the two yellow-haired, red-faced children. They were at opposite corners of the room bawling their eyes out. Their parents were nowhere to be seen. Edgar and Isabella had clearly argued about the small dog that was holding up its paw and whimpering in pain in the middle of the room. I guessed they'd fought over who should hold it, and now the poor thing was injured. They were too wrapped up in themselves to tend to it.

Edgar and Isabella were so childish, so downright silly, that Heathcliff and I started to laugh. We couldn't help ourselves. And they heard, and they were so terrified that both of them nearly soiled themselves in panic. That made us laugh even more. Then Heathcliff gave a ghostly wail and I scratched my nails down the windowpane to frighten the silly things out of their wits.

"We're lost souls," I wailed. "We've been wandering the moor these twenty years. Won't you let us in?"

I scraped the glass again.

They shrieked so loudly that their dear mama and papa came running.

"Ghosts! Evil spirits!" screamed Edgar and Isabella. But their parents did not believe that what was outside the window was anything other than human.

"Robbers!" said Mrs. Linton.

"Thieves! Cutthroats!" said Mr. Linton. He started yelling for the servants, and a moment later we heard a door being unbolted.

We fled and we would have gotten clean away had they not set the dogs on us.

A bulldog's bite is a terrible thing. When its jaws clamp together, they grip so hard it is impossible to pull them apart. I'd lost my shoes—my feet were bare. When the dog's teeth closed on my ankle, there was nothing at all to protect it. They punctured my flesh and I could feel muscle peeling from bone. I'd never felt pain like it. I fell flat on my face and the bulldog started dragging me back toward the house, snorting and slobbering. It shook me as if I were a piece of meat. I truly feared I was going to be eaten alive. Heathcliff grabbed a rock and tried to beat the dog off, but he could not get me free. He was swearing and cursing and the dog was growling, while a man shouted at it to hold me tight, to not let go. But when the man got nearer and held up his lantern, he gave a cry of shock and ordered the bulldog off.

Pain and loss of blood made me lose my senses. I must have fainted, because I remember nothing after that until I woke to find myself lying in a crimson room, staring up at a ceiling of gold and white. My head was spinning, but I was dimly aware of two golden-haired figures hovering close by. For a moment I thought I'd died and gone to Heaven. But if that was the case, why was I in such pain? Was this Hell?

There was a man standing nearby who smelled of stables and the outdoors. A great bulldog sat by his side. Behind me I heard Heathcliff cursing and a woman shrieking with horror at the foulness of his language. Someone else was threatening to lock Heathcliff in the cellar.

They'll have to catch him first, I thought. He'll lead them on a merry chase!

I turned my head toward Heathcliff and then I heard a boy saying, "That's Miss Earnshaw, Mother!"

Mrs. Linton took a closer look at me and decided her son was right. It didn't take the Lintons long to work out that Heathcliff was the "dirty Spanish castaway" that my father had brought home from Liverpool. They handed Heathcliff a lantern and thrust him out into the night, and I was too weak to object.

I was not myself at all. If I'd been myself, I'd have spat in Mrs. Linton's face when she took off my cloak. I'd have gone running after Heathcliff, but I could not stand, let alone walk. They had me trapped. And yet they were not treating me like a prisoner. Mrs. Linton held a glass of something warm and sweetly scented to my lips and told me to drink. I've no idea what was in it, but warmth spread into my veins and dulled the pain in my ankle. It made my head feel light, and a haze of contentment washed over me as if I were in a happy dream.

A maid came and gently—so gently!—washed my feet in warm water. She cleaned my wounds and bandaged my ankle. Then she dried my hair and combed it, taking time to ease out the tangles, not tugging and raking at it like Nelly did.

Edgar stood staring at me all the while, his eyes as big and bright as a puppy's. When the maid was done, he edged nearer and asked, "Does it hurt much?"

"Yes," I said. "It hurts like hell."

"But you didn't cry out," Edgar said. "Not once."

"What would be the point of that?" I replied.

Edgar's eyes got bigger and brighter. The expression in them was unfamiliar to me. I couldn't work out what was going on in his head at all.

Isabella came tiptoeing across the room then, carrying a plate of dainty cakes. I assumed she'd hog them to herself, that she'd stand there eating in front of me, teasing, watching my mouth water. Instead she put the whole plate in my lap and said, "Can you manage to eat something?"

Isabella had the same puppy-dog look on her face as her brother. Suddenly I pictured myself patting them both on the head. Would they roll over and show me their bellies? I smiled at the thought of it, catching Edgar's eye as I looked up. Color flooded across his face, turning his milk-white cheeks scarlet.

I was an intruder, yet they were behaving as if I were an invited guest. It was almost as if those two children liked me. Admired me, even. Me—who'd mocked them and banged on the windows to frighten them half to death. Could such a thing be possible?

Mr. Linton ordered a sofa to be pulled over to the fire. I assumed he and his wife would take their places on it, sucking up all the heat, leaving me in the corner to shiver like I did at home. But no. Wonder of wonders! Mr. Linton himself picked me up, carried me over to the sofa, and laid me down gently on the crimson cushions as if I were a princess he'd rescued from pirates.

The little dog Isabella and Edgar had been fighting over jumped up and settled down beside me. I smoothed its ears and it wagged its tail and licked my face. I held the dog to my chest, feeling its downy softness. I was so used to hunger and cold and cruelty and noise that I could hardly believe this quiet gentleness. It was so strange to me to be the focus of such attention, I didn't know how to behave. It was like moving from the darkest of winters into dazzling spring sunshine in the blink of an eye. Without Heathcliff to shield me, I was blinded by the glare.

7.

I was at Thrushcross Grange for five weeks. It might as well have been five years for the difference the Lintons made to me. In those five weeks I was transformed from urchin to lady. When I returned to Wuthering Heights, I was dressed in finery, primped and preened, my hair curled and dressed to within an inch of its life.

What had come over me? Was I so shallow that my heart and mind could be turned by such nonsense?

Of course not.

But I had seen that very first night what money could do. And I'd seen in Heathcliff's eyes what being poor and powerless was. I was a girl. I could not fight battles or plow fields. I could not make my own fortune. But perhaps I could marry one. I was twelve years old, but already I could feel there was power in my looks. I saw it in Edgar Linton's puppy-dog eyes every time he looked at me. It is not vanity but a mere statement of fact to say that I was superior to Isabella in face and figure. I intended to use what God had given me to my advantage.

It was Christmas Eve when I came back home. I thought Heathcliff would come running to meet me. But he did not. My brother lifted me down from my pony, admiring my looks and saying I'd become a lady. If I impressed Hindley, why, then, I could wind anyone around my finger.

We went into the house where Heathcliff skulked in the shadows. I flew across the floor when I saw him and flung my arms around his chest, kissing him so hard I made my lips bleed. I'd been starved, and now I could not have enough of him.

And yet Heathcliff stood as stiff as a post. His arms hung useless at his sides, he did not hold me hard to his chest and did not return my kisses.

What was wrong? I pulled back a little.

And suddenly I was embarrassed by my own happiness. Confused by his coldness. A gasp of hysteria came out of my throat that sounded almost like a laugh.

"Have you forgotten me?" I asked.

Heathcliff didn't answer. My blasted brother told Heathcliff he was permitted to shake hands with me, to greet me like the other servants had done. Hindley stood there smiling, sneering at Heathcliff's awkwardness. Frances was beside Hindley, holding back her giggles behind her hand. It was like a red rag to a bull.

"I'll not be laughed at!" Heathcliff said, and turned, but I caught him by the hand.

He was so filthy, so unkempt, I wondered what in the name of God my brother had been doing to him. I wanted to bathe Heathcliff's face, untangle the wild mane on his head. I said, "Have you not washed or brushed your hair these last five weeks?" They were such stupid words. Heathcliff thought I was mocking him too.

He shouted something—I don't remember exactly what. Some nonsense about liking to be dirty. Heathcliff snatched his hand away and ran from the room, with Hindley's laughter ringing in his ears. I would have followed, had I not been in that stupid dress, with skirts so long I could not run in them. I'd not a hope in hell of catching him. He'd run all the way to the cliffs, I thought. How long might it be before he came back?

My heart hurt and yet I would not let my brother see how badly I was wounded. I had to carry on smiling. I'd talk to Heathcliff later when I could get him on his own.

And so I played the game of being a lady. Edgar and Isabella had been invited to dine with us the following day, and Frances had acquired an array of trinkets to give them as gifts. I sat with Frances and cooed over their loveliness and decided which would be best for whom. And all the while we talked nonsense, I waited to hear Heathcliff's steps in the kitchen.

But he did not come home that night. And he was not there the following morning. I rode to church feeling crushed and miserable. When I prayed, I prayed only for Heathcliff. The rest of the world could go hang itself.

Edgar and Isabella came back with us after church, riding in their family's carriage. When we arrived at Wuthering Heights, I led them into the house and stood them in front of the fire. The fragile darlings were shivering from the cold.

And oh! How wonderful! Heathcliff was there—scrubbed and brushed and in clean clothes, looking magnificent. I was so very, very glad to see him! But before I could tell Heathcliff so, Hindley came in.

My brother began roaring, yelling at Heathcliff to be gone, to not show his face while we had guests. And when Heathcliff did not move, Hindley threatened to drag him out by the hair, shouting, "I'll pull those locks of yours even longer!"

"They're long enough already," Edgar said, the damned fool that he was. "They must make his head ache. It's a mane over his eyes." He laughed at his own joke.

Nelly had set food on the table before we'd come in. Heathcliff grabbed the first thing that came to hand, throwing a jug of hot applesauce into Edgar's face. Edgar began to scream like a baby and Isabella joined in with her brother, though nobody had laid a finger on her. Hindley was big and he was powerful. My brother snatched up Heathcliff, threw him over his back like he was a sack of wheat, and hoisted him up the stairs.

I knew what was coming. My fingers itched to slap Edgar. I had to ball my hands into fists to stop myself. "Why did you say that?" I asked him. "Hindley will beat Heathcliff now. I hate him being beaten. Why did you speak to him?"

Nelly was mopping sauce off Edgar's face. "I didn't speak to him," Edgar said. "I promised Mother I wouldn't. She said we were only allowed here if we didn't speak a word to that filthy brute." He started to snivel.

"Stop crying!" I told Edgar. "You're not killed. There's not even a mark on you. And you, Isabella. What are you bawling for? No one's hurt you!"

Their weeping and wailing continued until they heard Hindley's steps on the stairs. My brother came back in, flushed and cheerful after the beating he'd given Heathcliff. Hindley ordered us to the table, a great smile spread across his face. He began carving the goose, piling our plates, urging us to eat, drink, and be merry. Frances made such bright conversation that Isabella and Edgar recovered themselves perfectly. They had no care for Heathcliff and gave no thought as to how he suffered.

And me? I was in Hell. But I kept my face composed, I nodded and smiled when people expected me to. I made the right replies when called on to speak, but I could not manage to swallow a mouthful of the food. I was choked with hatred for my brother. And sick with sadness for Heathcliff's misery, for I felt it all. More than that even, I was enraged by my own weakness. I was twelve years old and could do nothing to help Heathcliff. Not yet.

8.

I was thirteen when Hindley's son was born. Hareton was a handsome baby, sturdy and strong. But it seemed all his mother's strength had gone into making him and Frances died not long after. My brother—who'd been brutal before—now became the very devil and Wuthering Heights the deepest pit of Hell. My lessons stopped. No one came near the house apart from Edgar, who'd rarely make the journey and only if Hindley was out drinking himself into oblivion.

Heathcliff took little satisfaction from Hindley's self-destruction. He feared my brother would kill himself before he had the chance to take his revenge.

I had no fondness for Hindley, none at all. I didn't much care what harm he did to himself. But I cared very much that he was dragging Heathcliff down with him.

Hindley reduced Heathcliff from servant to laborer. Every stinking task that no one else would do fell to him. Heathcliff worked from dawn to dusk, and when I did see him he was so tired he could barely say a word. He became the very brute Hindley had always called him.

I would have combed the tangles from Heathcliff's hair. I would have bathed his feet and scraped the muck from under his nails. I would have kissed away the pain of his blistered hands. But Heathcliff kept me at arm's length—if I tried to touch him he'd push me away. He was so sullen, so surly. Every day Heathcliff grew more distant from me and there was nothing I could do to bring him back. It grieved me beyond what I could bear. I could not understand it.

And then there was Edgar: a ray of sunlight shining into the darkness. Edgar, who would listen when I spoke, his head tilted to one side, an expression of deep concentration on his face. It was as if Edgar wanted every word of mine to become fixed in his mind like print on the page. He would gaze at me as if he were trying to paint my face inside his eyelids so that he could still see it when I was not there. There was an innocence to Edgar, a sweetness that made him seem like an illusion.

After he'd gone, I always felt I'd been dreaming and that I'd imagined him.

I'd first spoken to Edgar when I was twelve. For the three years after that I lived a kind of double life: there were two completely separate Catherine Earnshaws.

One went riding to Thrushcross Grange and bobbed and curtsied and was polite to Mr. Linton and his wife. That Catherine was kind to Isabella and utterly devoted to Edgar, taking great care that he should see no more than a fraction of what really lay in her mind and heart. She was meek and obedient and loving: the ladylike creature her parents had longed for.

The other Catherine Earnshaw lived at Wuthering Heights and witnessed daily scenes of such violence that she wondered if she would survive them.

9.

Edgar doted on me, but he always stopped short of declaring his love. Sometimes he seemed on the brink of it, but then his mother would come in or his sister would join us. Something always killed the words before they fell from his lips.

And then, one morning when I was fifteen years old, Hindley announced he must make the journey to Gimmerton, the nearest town. There was business that needed doing and he'd not be back until nightfall. This was my chance to get Edgar on his own. I scribbled a note for the baker's boy to carry to Thrushcross Grange and deliver into Edgar's hands. That afternoon I asked Nelly to make me smart enough to receive him.

She was brushing my hair when Heathcliff came in, stinking of pig muck, leaves in his hair, half a field under his fingernails. Heathcliff declared that, as Hindley was gone, he was going to have himself a day's rest.

The two Catherine Earnshaws collided. What was I to do? If I hadn't sent the note to Edgar, I'd have gladly run off on the moors with Heathcliff. But Edgar was coming.

Heathcliff had seen the dress I was wearing and the way Nelly was arranging my hair.

"Are you expecting visitors?" he asked. His voice was as rough as his looks.

"You cannot take a day off," I said. "Hindley will beat you when he finds out."

"He won't find out," Heathcliff replied. "There's no one to tell him."

"Edgar will be calling," I confessed.

"Have Nelly say you're busy. Don't turn me out for that pitiful friend of yours."

Suddenly Nelly's clumsy fiddling with my hair annoyed me. "Nelly!" I said. "Stop now. Leave me alone."

"Look there on the wall," Heathcliff said, and pointed to the calendar nailed to it. "I've marked a cross for the days you've spent with Edgar and a dot for the ones you've spent with me."

My throat tightened with guilt when I saw how Edgar's days outnumbered his. Heathcliff *had* noticed then, when I thought he didn't care a bit. He'd noticed. What did that mean? Words tumbled from my mouth before I could stop them, words that made no sense and did nothing but hurt both of us. "Why should I spend my time with you? You never have anything to say!"

If I'd been able to rake those words out of the air before they'd reached Heathcliff's ears, I'd have done so. The look on his face was terrible to see. And at that moment there was the clatter of a horse's hooves and Edgar was tapping gently on the door. He stepped in as Heathcliff stormed out.

"I'm not too early, am I?" Edgar asked. And his voice was as soft as a summer breeze. He was such a pale, wafting thing compared to Heathcliff! I felt torn apart. My heart was beating like mad, a sweat broke out on my brow. And there was Nelly, gaping, with Hareton clinging to her skirts. Nelly started dusting things frantically, making herself busy. She was enjoying this, damn her!

"What are you doing, Nelly?" I snapped. I was so upset, I couldn't be the Catherine Earnshaw I was supposed to be.

"I'm doing my work, miss," Nelly said. Her eyes were bugging out.

"We have company," I said. "Servants don't dust when we have guests in the room."

"Mr. Hindley hates me to be fidgeting around him dusting when he's at home," Nelly said. "It's a good opportunity while he's in Gimmerton. I'm sure Mr. Edgar won't mind."

"I don't like your fidgeting either," I said.

"That's a pity," Nelly replied, and carried on dusting.

I was in such a state that I lost my temper. I snatched the duster from her hand. I was itching to slap her and she could see it. Nelly smirked, and the rage I'd spent three years containing in Edgar's presence erupted. I pinched her. One small pinch, that was all. But Nelly yelped as if I'd knocked her head off.

"Oh, miss, what a nasty trick!" Nelly cried.

"I didn't touch you," I said.

"What's that then?" Nelly said, and rolled up her sleeve. She waved her arm in Edgar's face, showing off a huge purple bruise.

It was an old bruise, I'm sure of it. One tiny pinch couldn't have done that. But now I was so furious I slapped her face.

"Catherine, love! Catherine!" Edgar said. He'd never heard a raised voice in his life and was appalled. Any chance I'd had of Edgar declaring his love for me was gone. And it was Nelly's fault. I could happily have killed her.

"Leave the room, Nelly," I said.

Hareton began crying and I tried to stop his noise, for my head was aching. But he would not shut up, so I gave him a shake. And then Edgar tried to pull me off the little brat, and so I swung around. My fist collided with the side of Edgar's head.

Nelly picked up Hareton with a triumphant smile on her face. She sailed from the room, leaving me with Edgar—a pale, shivering rabbit of a man.

Edgar said nothing but picked up his hat and headed for the door.

"You're not going anywhere," I said.

"I must and I shall," Edgar replied.

"No." I barred his way. "Not yet. You'll not leave me like this. I'll be miserable after, and I won't be miserable for you."

"Can I stay after you've struck me?" Edgar asked. His eyes wouldn't meet mine. "You've made me afraid and ashamed of you. I'll not come here again."

Edgar was too well bred to slam the door. He went as quietly as he'd come. Three years of being polite and ladylike washed away in an instant. Three years of plotting and planning. And I was so drained by them! So tired of being the person Edgar wanted me to be! I was overcome with terrible sadness—not for Edgar but for what I'd said to Heathcliff. Why had he marked the calendar like that? Why had he said nothing until now? I'd thought Heathcliff didn't care for my company anymore. Was I wrong? I began to cry. In hurting Heathcliff, I'd hurt myself. I did not cry quietly or daintily. Great choking sobs ripped from my chest and I felt like I'd never stop.

I had no idea Edgar had heard me or that he'd stopped in the yard until I heard Nelly calling out to him.

"Miss Catherine is dreadfully wicked, sir. You'd best ride home."

Her words had the opposite effect to what she'd intended.

Edgar turned on his heel and came back in. My storm of tears took a long time to subside. He sat beside me, cradling me in his arms, kissing my hair, whispering soothing words into my ear. Edgar thought Heathcliff had caused my ill temper. He believed I was ashamed of myself and I was miserable because I regretted my outlandish behavior. Edgar thought I wept for fear of losing him. And I let him think those things. The more I cried for Heathcliff, the more in love Edgar thought I was with him. The more I raged about how Heathcliff had been treated, the more Edgar professed his love for me. By the time Hindley came storming home—crazed, drunk, and screaming for someone to beat—Edgar had asked me to be his wife.

10.

At the first sound of Hindley's homecoming, Edgar fled for his horse and I fled to my chamber. I could hear everything that followed through the floorboards.

Hareton was terrified of his father. It was Nelly's habit to hide him away when Hindley came home, but that night she did not do it fast enough. Hindley caught her in the act and all hell broke loose. He grabbed Nelly first and threatened her with a carving knife.

Then Hindley lost interest in killing Nelly and turned his attention on his son. He tried to cuddle the boy, but Hareton wriggled and wailed as if everything in Hell was after him. Hindley's mood switched once more. He decided Hareton was a changeling in need of a haircut. Hindley carried his son up the stairs to find a pair of scissors. At that moment, Heathcliff came in and Hindley swung around. Hareton made one last attempt to break free and slipped from his father's grasp, tumbling over the bannister.

The boy's brains would have been dashed out on the flagstone floor below had not Heathcliff caught him.

Hindley must have seen how close he'd come to killing his son, despite his drunkenness. He left Hareton alone after that. Hindley went back down the stairs, took more brandy from the dresser, and then retired to his room to drink himself into a stupor.

Nelly sat trying to soothe the terrified, whimpering child.

I had a sudden, desperate desire to be soothed too. I was so very troubled. I had succeeded in the plan I'd made at twelve years old. But now, at fifteen, the plan did not look quite so simple as it had then. The day's events weighed on my chest like a millstone. If I didn't ease the weight by talking to another human soul, my ribs would be crushed. There was no one but Nelly. She'd have to do.

I tiptoed downstairs and put my head around the door. "Are you alone, Nelly?" I asked.

"Yes, miss." Nelly replied gently so as not to disturb Hareton, but her face was far from welcoming.

"Where's Heathcliff?" I said.

Nelly told me he was in the stables, working. And then she sat, as still as stone, her lips clenched tight. Did Nelly have no sympathy for me? No pity? I felt my tears begin to flow. "I'm very unhappy," I said.

Nelly grunted. "So many friends and so few cares and yet you can't make yourself content!"

Few cares? I almost laughed out loud. Had Nelly forgotten the evening's events? Had she wiped from her mind the scenes of horror performed in this house every day of the week? My brother was an ugly, raging drunk. Did she not see how Heathcliff suffered at his hands? How could she think I had no cares? The woman was an idiot! And yet still I needed to talk. "Will you keep a secret for me?" I asked.

Nelly looked up. She liked a secret and the idea that I'd give her one of mine snagged her like a fish on a hook. "Is it worth keeping?" she said.

"Yes," I replied. "And it worries me so much I must let it out. Edgar has asked me to marry him. I've given him an answer. But tell me—what should I have said? Yes or no?"

Nelly's eyebrows shot almost to the ceiling. "After your display of temper this afternoon?" she said. “Edgar must be hopelessly stupid or willfully reckless.”

“He’s neither,” I told her. “I said yes.”

“You’ve given your word then,” Nelly sniffed. “There’s no getting out of it now. What more is there to be said on the matter?”

“There is so much more! Have I done right?”

“Do you love him?” Nelly asked.

“Of course,” I said. Edgar was so eager to please, he tried so hard to make me happy, he gave so much and asked for so little. It was as easy to love Edgar as it was to love a puppy.

“Well, your brother will be pleased, I suppose,” Nelly said. “He’ll have you off his hands and you’ll escape this hellhole. So why are you unhappy? Where’s the problem?”

I slapped my forehead. “Here,” I said. I struck my chest. “And here. Wherever the soul lives. In my heart and soul I know it’s wrong.”

I paused a while, then said, “I had a dream last night, Nelly. I’d died and gone to Heaven and I was so very miserable up there that I cried and cried. And at last the angels got sick of hearing me and threw me out. I landed on the moor near Wuthering Heights and I woke up sobbing for joy. I’ve no more right to marry Edgar Linton than

I have to be in Heaven. If my blasted brother hadn't brought Heathcliff so low, I'd never even have thought of it. It would degrade me to marry Heathcliff now." I sighed and wiped the tears that spilled down my cheeks. "So Heathcliff will never know how much I love him. Not because he's handsome but because he's more myself than I am. Whatever our souls are made from, Heathcliff's and mine are the same. But Edgar's soul is as different from mine as frost is from fire."

"Have you thought how Heathcliff will take the marriage?" Nelly asked.

Of course I'd thought of it! I never thought of anything else. I'd decided that my marriage would not give him pain. Heathcliff had been so cold these last few months, so locked within himself. He would not be hurt but helped by it—it would rescue him from the prison he'd built around himself. I'd thought this only yesterday. But today I'd seen Heathcliff's marks on the calendar. Tormented, I said to Nelly, "Heathcliff has no idea of these things, does he? He does not know what being in love is."

"You think not?" Nelly said. "When you become Catherine Linton, Heathcliff will lose his friend, love, everything. He'll be deserted and alone in the world."

I laughed aloud at that idea. "Heathcliff deserted?" I said. "Alone? The two of us, separated? Who would have the power to do that? I'll never leave Heathcliff, never! He'll be as much with me as he always has been. Edgar must learn to tolerate him. If I married Heathcliff, we'd be beggars. We'd starve. But when I marry Edgar, I can help Heathcliff. I can free him from my brother's grip, set him on his own two feet, help him be the man he was meant to be."

Nelly was aghast. "You'll use your husband's money?" she said. "That's as poor a reason to get married as I ever heard."

"It is the best!" I told her. "I do not marry for my pleasure—there is no selfishness in this! I am marrying Edgar for Heathcliff. I see no other way to help him."

Nelly gave me such a look that I had to explain myself. "Nelly, what would be the use of me if all I am is within this body? I have watched and felt all of Heathcliff's miseries from the beginning. My only purpose in living is him. If all else perished and Heathcliff remained, I should still continue to be. And if all else remained and Heathcliff were destroyed, the universe would turn into a mighty stranger—I would not be part of it. My love for

Edgar is like the leaves in the woods. Time will change it as winter changes the trees. My love for Heathcliff is like the eternal rocks beneath—an unseen delight perhaps, but necessary. Nelly, I am Heathcliff. He's always, always in my mind—not as a pleasure, any more than I am always a pleasure to myself, but as my own being. So don't talk of our separation again. It is impossible."

I wished I had not bothered, for Nelly looked at me as if I'd told her I was to be the bride of Satan. And I had not said the half of it. I could hardly admit to myself the dark thought that lingered at the back of my head: that people close to me died. They died all the time. Mother. Father. Frances. And Edgar was such a pale, weak thing: I'd surely outlive him. And then when Edgar died? I'd be rich. Free. I could do whatever I chose.

If I told Nelly that, she'd have died of shock on the spot. Already she was saying, "Either you do not know what it is to be a wife or you're a wicked, devious girl. Don't tell me any more of your secrets. I won't keep them."

Nelly said no more, for the kitchen door opened and the farmhands came in for their supper. Nelly handed me Hareton to mind while she fetched them food. The farmhands ate, but Heathcliff did not join them. Nelly went to the stable to fetch him in, but she came back alone.

And only then did she whisper to me that Heathcliff had been sitting in the high-backed chair when Nelly and I had been talking, where I could not see him. He'd heard me say it would degrade me to marry him, but no more, for at that moment he'd left the room.

I cannot begin to describe the horror I felt. I went dashing out into the night, hysterical. I screamed and screamed his name, and when Heathcliff did not answer I ran back to the house and told Nelly to send the farmhands after him. He must be brought back. He must. I needed to speak to him.

They could find no trace of him. A storm was gathering and Nelly said the rain would bring Heathcliff home, but it did not. And so I went out again, running, walking, staggering along the road calling his name. I kept on until I was soaked to the skin and my teeth chattered so hard I could call no more.

By the time I got back home, Nelly had gone to bed. But I could not. I sat and waited and the fire died and so did the storm and still Heathcliff did not come. I sat there until the first rays of the morning sun woke my brother and he came down the stairs to find me sitting wet and cold and sick with grieving.

I cannot say what happened after that. I took a fever and the days and nights that followed were a blur of utter misery. I was really dreadfully ill for a very long time. I'm told Edgar's mother came calling and that when I was strong enough to be moved she carried me off to Thrushcross Grange to recover, but I have no memory of it. Perhaps it's just as well. Mrs. Linton caught the fever from me and did not recover as I did. And nor did her husband. By the time I returned to Wuthering Heights, Edgar and Isabella Linton were orphans.

11.

Three years passed. Three years in which I heard not a word from Heathcliff. There was no message carried by the baker's boy. No letter. No note. Nothing. It drove me out of my mind—to be left utterly in the dark, to not know what Heathcliff did, what he thought, what he felt, what he suffered, whether he lived or died even. I could not rest or be active—nothing stopped the missing of him itching under my skin until I wanted to peel it off my bones. I was in agony every waking moment, and when I slept I dreamed of him. I was being tortured on a rack and there seemed no end to the pain.

And so, in the presence of God and before witnesses, I promised to love, honor, and obey Edgar Linton until death do us part. There seemed nothing else to do but marry him.

Nelly had been right—I did not know what it was to be a wife. I had no mother to explain what would be expected of me. I must endure Edgar's caresses. I must welcome him into my bed and suffer his touch. But the only person's hands I wanted on my flesh were Heathcliff's.

Hindley had decided he wanted no more women in the house once I was gone. He sent Nelly along with me to live at Thrushcross Grange. Hareton, five years old and still mortally afraid of his father, was left alone with the monster.

I didn't want Nelly with me. I'd never forgiven her for her silence that night. If she'd spoken sooner, I'd have caught up with Heathcliff. I'd have gone with him wherever he led. I would have thrown myself under his horse before I'd let him leave without me. But Nelly came to Thrushcross Grange, for I had not the strength to object. I'd long since recovered from the fever in my body, but I still suffered from a sickness of the mind. My spirits were so depressed that the world was drab and colorless. Edgar was kindness itself, but despite all his efforts I could care about nothing.

When tradesmen came to the kitchen door, I sometimes heard Nelly telling them how contented the newlyweds were. She said we were in possession of a deep and growing happiness.

I would have roared with laughter every time I overheard that, if I had the energy to do so.

I wanted to say, "Nelly Dean, you are a fool! Could anybody be more wrong? I'd once felt too big, too wild to be held in so small a thing as a body, but I am a shriveled, pitiful creature now. Can you not see that? Heathcliff's absence has not just halved me, it's reduced me to nothing. I'm rattling around inside my ribs like a pea in an empty barrel!"

There were times I wanted to rage and storm. Times I tried to provoke Edgar just so I'd have something to lash out against. It would at least prove that I existed. But Edgar had such a fear of my temper, he would bend to me like a blade of grass in the wind. He tiptoed around me, fulfilling my every whim, treating me like a sick child. And indeed, I was crippled—weak with a sorrow that I could not even begin to describe.

How could that be mistaken for happiness?

How could that be called contentment?

But Nelly did not see *me*. Nor did Edgar or Isabella. The only person who had ever seen me was Heathcliff. And without him as my mirror, I could not even see myself.

12.

Edgar and I had been married six months. It was early autumn. Evening. I was sitting with Edgar in the window seat of the crimson drawing room. The sun's dying rays cast a golden light on the gardens, where Nature had been tamed. Everything was pruned and clipped and cut so brutally that it made me shudder. The gardens held nothing that pleased my eye. Instead my gaze was drawn beyond the walls to the rise of hill and moor. Just over that ridge lay Wuthering Heights. Four miles distant but a world away now. I was wishing Heathcliff and I had never run through the dark that night, that we'd never stood and peered into this very window. I wished that we'd never frightened Edgar and his sister, that we'd never gotten caught. I was so sad, thinking how things might have turned out if we'd only followed a different path.

I was pregnant with Edgar's child by then, though I did not know it yet, and it had made me dreadfully weary. My husband took my silence for calm and smiled tenderly at me while remarking on the beauty of the evening. I forced myself to return his smile. It seemed a huge effort to arrange my face so, but Edgar didn't see how much it cost me and that made me even sadder.

Nelly came in to light the candles. I was dimly aware that she was on edge, as if something had upset her, but I cared nothing for Nelly's troubles. As she turned to go, she muttered suddenly, "A person from Gimmerton wishes to see you, ma'am."

"What does he want?" I said.

"I didn't ask."

A tradesman, I assumed. As mistress of a big house, I had an endless stream of dull, humdrum matters to deal with.

"Close the curtains then," I told Nelly. "Bring up tea. I'll be back in a moment, Edgar."

I had no relish for the task ahead and walked slowly from the room, along the passage, through the kitchen, and out of the back door. I could see no one in the courtyard and I was about to sigh with irritation, thinking that the wretched tradesman had not bothered to wait.

I inhaled a deep breath and—oh God!—my heart stopped beating.

Time halted.

The world tilted on its axis.

I could taste something in the air. It caught at the back of my throat—a scent so familiar it brought tears rushing to my eyes and a name bursting from my lips.

"Heathcliff?"

It could not be him. I had lost my mind—this was some delicious delusion. Oh, I wished it would last forever! I spun around. There was nothing. Was he a ghost, then? Had Heathcliff died and come to take his leave?

"Heathcliff!" I called again. As if I had conjured him into being, he stepped from the shadows. There he stood.

Tall. Handsome. The man he was meant to be.

And he'd done it without my help.

Heathcliff. My Heathcliff.

Three years of missing him. Three years of longing for him. Three years of agony. The pain balled itself up in my chest and broke out of my throat. I made a sound that was barely human. A cry from the very depths of my being. My shout split the night, banging between the hills, echoing from Thrushcross Grange to Wuthering Heights and back again. And then Heathcliff was there, his arms around me, and he was warm and solid and real and alive.

His breath was hot on my neck as he held me and said, "I feared you had forgotten me, Cathy."

"Never! Never! Never!" I told him.

The noise I'd made had caught Edgar's attention. I heard a window being opened and then Edgar calling out to me, "Don't stand outside, love! Bring the person in if it's anyone particular."

I took Heathcliff's hand in mine and said, "Come in, come in."

"I doubt your husband will welcome me with the same passion you do, Cathy," Heathcliff said. "Should you not tell him it's me?"

I flew back to the drawing room. My joy was so great that I flung my arms around Edgar's neck and shrieked in his ear, "It's Heathcliff. He's come back!"

"There's no need to strangle me," Edgar said. "He's surely not worth this amount of fuss. There's no need to be so frantic."

"Oh, I know you never much liked Heathcliff," I said. Edgar's irritation did nothing to dent my happiness. "But you must be friends now, for my sake. Can I tell him to come up?"

"Here?" Edgar said, aghast.

"Where else?" I asked.

"Surely the kitchen would be more appropriate?"

"You'd have your wife sit in the kitchen, would you?" I said, teasing Edgar for his foolishness. He didn't answer. "Nelly, set two tables in here," I continued. "Edgar and Isabella can drink their tea at one, since they're gentry. Heathcliff and I will sit at the other table, as we're of the lower orders. Will that suffice, darling? Or must I take Heathcliff to another room altogether? Tell Nelly what you want, I'm off to fetch Heathcliff indoors."

Edgar caught my wrist to stop me. "Nelly will bring him up," Edgar said, waving her out of the door. "You are mistress of Thrushcross Grange. The whole house need not witness the sight of you welcoming a runaway servant as a brother."

That pulled me up short. "A runaway servant?" I echoed.

"He is a nobody," Edgar said. "A plowboy!"

"I'll not have you call him such things," I replied. "Heathcliff is dearer to me than you can imagine and nothing you say or do will change that. Do you not see how happy I am? If you loved me, you'd welcome his return as much as I do."

"I cannot," Edgar said.

"Well, then. You have a choice. You welcome Heathcliff into our home or I will leave it now along with him. And what will the servants say about that, I wonder?"

Heathcliff was at the door then, being shown in by Nelly. The change in him made Edgar's eyes almost pop out of his head. Heathcliff was no plowboy but a man as well dressed, as well groomed as Edgar was. He stood a whole head taller, with shoulders twice as wide. Heathcliff had become a gentleman, and beside him Edgar looked like a schoolboy. I took pity on my husband then. The poor darling looked so miserable and I hated to see him unhappy. I was so full of joy I wanted Edgar to share in it. I ran across the room, took Heathcliff's arm in mine, and led him over to Edgar. I made them shake hands like civilized human beings.

There was a silence which Edgar at last broke, saying stiffly, "Sit down, sir. My wife wishes me to welcome you and I, of course, am glad when anything pleases her."

"I too," said Heathcliff. "Especially if it's anything in which I have a part. I shall stay an hour or two most willingly."

Gone was the sullen, silent brute of a boy who could not string a sentence together unless it was to curse my brother. Heathcliff took a seat opposite me, and Edgar made a brave effort at conversation. He spoke of politics and world affairs. He mentioned books he'd read. He quoted poetry. If Edgar hoped to expose Heathcliff's lack of education, he was sorely disappointed. Heathcliff did not say what he had been doing with himself and how he'd earned such money to effect his transformation. Yet it was evident that Heathcliff knew more, was better read, and was more widely traveled than my husband. The men talked on, but I recall little of it. I cared nothing for the affairs of men or Heathcliff's past. All that mattered was he was here, now, in front of me. My eyes were drinking Heathcliff in after three years of drought. I sucked in every last detail. The way his hair curled at the nape of his neck. His hands—soft, clean, the nails trimmed, but with calluses that were evidence of hard work. There was a scar across his cheek that had not been there before.

As they spoke, Heathcliff's eyes were lowered to the floor, glancing my way just once or twice. Then, as Heathcliff began to relax, he looked at me more often. And then he stopped talking altogether and gazed. I saw every morsel of my delight shining back at me in his beautiful crow-black eyes.

Heathcliff and I sat in silence for a long time, simply smiling at one another. I've no idea what Edgar did—for us he no longer existed. At last I could stay still no more. I stepped across the rug, kneeled at Heathcliff's feet, and grasped his hands.

"I shall think this a dream tomorrow," I said. "I shall not be able to believe that I've seen you and touched you and spoken to you once more. And yet, cruel Heathcliff, you don't deserve this welcome. To be absent and silent for three years! Three years, and you never thought of me?"

"I've thought of you more often than you've thought of me, I'll wager," Heathcliff replied. "I heard of your marriage not long since, Cathy. I came here only to have one last glimpse of your face. But this welcome has put that idea from my mind. You'll not drive me off again. You were truly sorry I left, were you? Feared for me, did you? Well, you had good cause to. I've lived a hard and bitter life since last I heard your voice. But all those struggles, all those hardships—I suffered them only for you."

Edgar's voice sliced between us like a knife, icily polite. "Catherine, unless we are to drink cold tea, please come to the table. Mr. Heathcliff will have a long walk to wherever he lodges tonight and I'm thirsty."

Edgar sounded so sullen, so jealous and childish, that I pitied the poor darling. As I was an obedient wife, I did as I was told. The moment Isabella joined us, I poured the tea. But I did not drink a drop and I ate nothing.

Heathcliff was the only nourishment I needed.

13.

Poor Edgar. He was so shocked by the difference in me. He'd rescued me as a drowning kitten and now I'd grown into a tigress overnight. I was whole again, restored, my soul so magnified that it strained against the confines of my body.

Edgar wore himself out with jealousy after Heathcliff left that evening, weeping and sulking. He could not bear for me to be delighted with anyone who was not him. I pitied my husband. He was like a bird with a broken wing: miserable and helpless, not understanding the calamity it has suffered, only wanting the pain to go away. I could no more stand to see Edgar unhappy than I could bear to see a darling child weep.

The following morning, I was so gentle, so tender and affectionate, that I restored Edgar to good spirits. I made such a fuss of him that in the afternoon he allowed me to go to Wuthering

Heights to call on Heathcliff. To be respectable, Edgar insisted Isabella go along with me.

When we arrived at the Heights, I discovered that Hindley had invited Heathcliff to stay on as his guest. I knew full well that Heathcliff intended to take revenge on my brother, but Hindley was so depraved himself, he could not see the danger he was in.

We did not stay long inside the house. Instead Heathcliff and I walked the old, familiar path to the cliffs, with Isabella running on ahead, exclaiming about the wonderful view. While she was out of earshot I made one request of Heathcliff. I asked that he do my brother no bodily harm, nothing that Heathcliff might be punished for. "You mustn't hang for him," I said. "I could not bear to see you dangling at the end of a rope."

"I won't." Heathcliff grinned, a wild, wolfish smile. "It's true enough, I planned to kill Hindley. These three years I've imagined it in every detail. I was going to take one last look at you. If I found you'd forgotten me, I'd have come here and done the deed. And after that I'd have done away with myself so the law couldn't have me. Your welcome put an end to that plan and now I wish to live. But I warn you, Cathy, I will have justice."

I said nothing more. Hindley had been the cause of Heathcliff's degradation. Whatever was coming to him, I was sure that my brother deserved it.

14.

Heathcliff was slow to make a return visit to Thrushcross Grange. When he did, he trod very carefully. Heathcliff had always been good at hiding the depth of his feelings, and in Edgar's company he did so perfectly. He was well-mannered. Courteous. Constrained. Heathcliff behaved to me like a loving brother. A gentleman. Before very long, Heathcliff was calling so frequently that Edgar stopped remarking on it. He was not exactly a welcome visitor, but he was tolerated.

Weeks passed. Then months. It was as if I walked a tightrope between Edgar and Heathcliff. Every day it was harder to keep my balance. When I told Edgar I was with child, he was overjoyed. But I saw the looks Heathcliff gave my swelling belly. I knew how violently he resented Edgar, the man who'd planted the child there. I know Heathcliff thought of my baby as an unwelcome parasite. I also saw the sideways glances Heathcliff gave Edgar and knew what the sudden twitching of his fingers meant. Heathcliff looked that way at Hindley too. He was longing to do damage to my husband, but for my sake he would not. And so I ignored every dark look. I told myself that I was happy, that we were in a state of peaceful content. But really it was as if the three of us were sitting on a barrel of gunpowder. Sooner or later it had to explode.

Isabella was the spark.

Isabella. My sister-in-law. Just a year younger than me but still such a child! All her life she'd been so spoiled, so protected, that she knew nothing of the world or its wicked ways. Silly, silly Isabella suddenly developed the most ridiculous passion for Heathcliff. She couldn't eat or sleep, so great was her infatuation.

It was totally uninvited and wholly unprovoked. Indeed, it was so unlikely that Edgar and I had not the slightest idea what was troubling Isabella. Heathcliff had given her no reason whatsoever to inspire her passion. He never spoke to Isabella or even looked her way. To him she was of less interest than a bucket, for at least a bucket was useful.

The entire household noticed there was something wrong with Isabella. She was cross and quarrelsome with the servants and so unlike herself I thought she must be ill.

One evening Edgar was away and I was left alone with Isabella. She became particularly whiny and fretful. Nothing I could say or do would please her. In the end I told her to go to bed early and that in the morning I'd send for the doctor. She suddenly turned on me. It was all my fault, she declared. I was the reason she was ill. I was making her miserable.

Her attack was so sudden, so startling, that for a moment I was lost for words. "How so?" I asked.

An outburst poured from her mouth. Isabella complained that the previous day when we'd been out walking on the moor I'd sent her away.

"I did no such thing," I said. "I told you only to go where you pleased. Heathcliff and I were talking of the past. I did not want you bored, and there was nothing in our conversation to interest you."

"You did it so you could have him all to yourself," Isabella said. "You're so greedy. You hog all his attention and will not let me get near him. Everyone must worship you! But I'm worthy of love too!"

Isabella's secret came tumbling out then. She declared she loved Heathcliff with a passion far greater than Edgar had for me. She was sure that Heathcliff would love her back if only I didn't keep getting in her way!

How she ran on! I listened, amazed. Somehow she'd talked herself into believing that Heathcliff's rough exterior hid a noble mind, a poetic soul, and a tender, loving heart. The silly girl had created a perfect fairy-tale prince out of a man I knew to be as hard as granite. Heathcliff had good reason to be the way he was—I don't blame him for it. But I knew he would crush Isabella like a robin's egg if he ever had her in his power!

So I told Isabella of Heathcliff's nature. I was honest with her as I never had been with Edgar. She did not believe me. She called me a selfish hog. A poisonous friend.

I should have left her to it. Her "love" would have faded in time. But Isabella angered me so much I was not thinking straight.

The following day, she and I were sitting in the library, silent, but both of us festering with dreadful bad tempers, when Heathcliff came calling.

Isabella's obsession with him was a thing that had grown in the dark, I thought. I was sure that if it was exposed to the light of day, it would crumble to dust.

I welcomed Heathcliff and told him I'd found someone who doted on him more than I did, intending to be playful. I said Isabella and I had been fighting like cats over him. I told him she was dying of love for a man so physically and morally perfect.

Heathcliff looked at Isabella then for the first time, and his hatred of her Linton blood was clear in every line in his face. He couldn't have looked more disgusted had she been a slug. Isabella ran from the room in tears.

After she'd left, Heathcliff asked me if I was serious. He laughed long and loud at her silliness. Heathcliff called her all kinds of names and said how much he despised her. I thought that would be the end of it.

With Isabella gone and Edgar away from home, Heathcliff and I could talk freely. I asked after Hindley, and Heathcliff told me that gambling had been added to my brother's list of vices. Hindley was losing money hand over fist to Heathcliff, but he could no more stop himself gambling than he could stop himself drinking.

"And Hareton?" I asked. "How does he manage?"

"I stand between him and his father," Heathcliff replied. "The boy loves me for it and curses his 'devil daddy.'"

"And do you love Hareton back?" I asked.

A sneer curled Heathcliff's lip. He said only, "He is Hindley's child," and then he changed the subject.

Much later, as Heathcliff was preparing to leave, he asked, "Isabella . . . is she her brother's heir?"

"No," I said and patted my belly. "Not if this is a boy."

I gave the silly girl no more thought. But Heathcliff did. I'd planted the idea in his mind and it grew. Even if Isabella did not inherit the house, she would have money when she came of age. Heathcliff knew too well what it was to be poor and powerless. Besides that, how it would pain Edgar if his darling sister married a plowboy such as Heathcliff! Isabella was a temptation Heathcliff could not resist.

15.

It was Nelly who brought matters to a head. Once again, Nelly was the cause of the crisis. How long had she watched? How long had she waited? How much had she yearned to set the whole thing on fire?

I came into the kitchen one evening and saw Nelly standing by the window, hunched by the side, staring out slyly as if not wanting to be seen. Nelly was so transfixed by something in the courtyard that she did not hear me come in.

"Judas!" Nelly muttered. "Traitor!"

"Who is, Nelly?" I asked.

She almost leaped out of her skin. But she soon recovered and fluffed up like a chicken with moral fury.

"Your so-called friend," Nelly said primly. "Ah! He sees me looking. He's coming in. How's he going to explain himself, I wonder? Sneaking around kissing Miss Isabella when he thought no one was watching."

Heathcliff entered the kitchen. He had the grace to look a little ashamed.

"What's this?" I asked him. "Are you tired of being welcomed here? Do you want Edgar bolting the doors against you?"

Bang. The barrel of gunpowder we'd been sitting on these last few months exploded.

"Bolt the doors against me?" Heathcliff replied, his rage unleashed. "I'd like to see him try. Every day I pray for a chance to speed your husband on his way to Heaven."

My rage rose to meet his. "You must leave Isabella alone!" I said.

"Can I not kiss her when she begs me to?" Heathcliff asked. "I'm not your husband—you needn't be jealous."

"I'm not!" I lied. "If you love Isabella, you shall marry her. But do you? I think you do not. You told me yourself you despise her."

"What do you care how I feel about her or anyone else?" Heathcliff said. "I've had enough. You've treated me damnably, Cathy. Damnably! Do you hear? And if you think I'm so dim-witted I can't see it, you're a fool. I can't be soothed with your sweet words, and if you think I won't take revenge, you're an idiot."

"I've treated you damnably? How have I?" I asked.

"We could have had a palace, you and I. But you flattened it to the ground. You built a hovel in its place. You admire yourself for your generosity in allowing me to live there. You feast and throw me crumbs from the table and expect me to be grateful!"

"You want revenge?" I said.

"Not on you. Never on you. You're welcome to torture me to death for your own amusement. We both know a tyrant beats his slaves, yet they never turn on him. Instead, the slaves crush those beneath them. Thank you for telling me Isabella's secret. I intend to make use of it."

"Why must you do that?" I asked. "Do peace and harmony bore you? Edgar has been in good temper, you could come and go as you pleased. Were we too peaceful, that you want a fight? You will destroy everything! Well, do it if you must. Quarrel with Edgar. Trick his sister. That's the perfect way to take revenge on me."

"Don't act the wounded innocent. This is your doing, Cathy," Heathcliff raged on. "Your heart is as deep as mine. Why did you pour your love into so small a vessel as Edgar Linton?! You might as well try to hold the ocean in a horse trough. You knew Edgar could not love you in eighty years as much as I could in a single day! And yet you chose that coward and expect me to be content? Do you know how much I yearn to pull out that golden hair of his? To peel off his milk-white skin? I'd offer to paint this house with his blood if I thought I could squeeze more than a teaspoon from his miserable body."

Nelly must have slipped out of the kitchen, but I was not aware of it until she came back. Edgar was with her. He looked at me, the very model of respectability, just like his father. My husband was shocked to the core. Not with Heathcliff, for he already knew him to be a lost cause. With me.

"Why do you remain here when he uses such language, Catherine?" Edgar said. "Are you so hardened that it does not shock you?"

Until that moment, I'd been ready to defend Edgar. I'd been about to demand that Heathcliff swear he would not harm a hair on my husband's head. But now suddenly I felt that I was looking at an enemy.

"Have you been listening at the door, Edgar?" I asked.

Heathcliff laughed.

Edgar drew himself up to his full height. He was still a head shorter than Heathcliff.

"I've tolerated you, sir," Edgar said, "not because I didn't know your bad character but because Catherine wished to keep up your friendship. I was foolish to allow it. You are poison, and from this day forward you will not be admitted to this house. You will leave now, by force if necessary."

Heathcliff looked Edgar up and down with a sneer on his face. "Cathy, this lamb of yours roars like a bull," he said. "He might just split his skull against my knuckles. What a shame he's not worth knocking down."

Edgar nodded at Nelly, and she made for the door. I guessed then that Edgar had men somewhere close by, lingering in the passage. I grabbed Nelly's arm, pulled her back in, and locked the door. Edgar was aghast.

"If you have not the courage to fight him," I told Edgar, "then make an apology. Don't pretend more courage than you possess."

Edgar tried to take the key from me, but I threw it into the fire. And then my brave, valiant husband collapsed into a chair and covered his face with his hands. Edgar was whimpering, trembling from head to toe.

"Oh dear! Are you defeated?" I said. "Don't fret. Heathcliff is as likely to sully his fists with your blood as the king is to march his army against a nest of mice."

"Cathy, you preferred this slobbering, shivering thing to me?" said Heathcliff. "I wish you joy with the coward. Is he weeping? Or is he going to faint with terror?"

Heathcliff walked over to the chair for a look. And Edgar, fearing for his life, I suppose, suddenly sprang up and lashed out blindly. By pure chance Edgar managed to punch Heathcliff so hard and fast in the throat that he could not breathe. And then my hero of a husband fled across the kitchen and out through the back door into the courtyard, calling all the while for help.

Bulldogs would be the least of Heathcliff's problems.

"Get away now," I told Heathcliff. "Edgar will come back with a dozen men."

“With that blow burning in my gullet?” Heathcliff said. “Hell, no. I’ll crush his ribs first.”

“No, Heathcliff. They’ll have knives. Guns. They’ll kill you. I could not bear it. Go. For my sake, go.”

And because I had asked him, Heathcliff left, taking my heart and soul with him. And the greater part of my mind.

16.

I could not bear it.

I could not bear it.

I could not bear it.

I hit my head on the wooden arm of the sofa over and over, but I could not drive the horror from my mind. My world had just exploded, smashing into smithereens that flew so far and wide there could be no mending it. Heathcliff was gone and it was unbearable.

So I did not bear it.

I broke. I fractured into pieces.

That night marked the end of me. My body lingered on some two months longer, but the Cathy I had been perished.

I was incoherent. I know that. I don't remember much of it. Brief flashes, that's all. I tore pillows with my teeth. I looked in the mirror and did not recognize the face I saw there. I didn't eat, for Heathcliff had once said he could not stand to see me hungry and so some part of me reasoned if I did not eat he would have to come back. But he did not come. And nor did Edgar. I was alone in my room and nobody cared. Things were so very wrong and I was the cause. My own monstrous stupidity rose up like a vampire and sucked the sanity from me.

Even so, I might have lived had Nelly not been sure that I was imagining the brain fever that took hold of me that night. She thought my ravings were a wicked pretense to frighten my husband and bend him to my will. So Nelly did not inform Edgar I was sick, only that I was sulking in my room and wouldn't come out. He brooded miserably in the library, and no doctor was sent for until it was too late.

While I was tormented by the most dreadful dreams and visions, Heathcliff and Isabella eloped. Foolish, foolish girl! She regretted it before a day had passed, for she quickly discovered I had been telling the truth about Heathcliff's nature.

Edgar would have nothing more to do with her—he never saw his sister again. But Nelly did. Two months after Heathcliff and Isabella had run away, the newlyweds came back to Wuthering Heights and Nelly called on Isabella.

Through Nelly, Heathcliff discovered I was sick. He talked Nelly into sneaking him into Thrushcross Grange when Edgar was out so he could see me.

And that I do remember. I remember every detail. Edgar had gone to church and I was glad of it. These last weeks he had watched me constantly, his wide eyes brimming with tears of pity. Edgar had given me such tender care, and I did not like to hurt him. But I did not want to see his face. I did not want to hear his voice. I did not want to feel his fingers caressing my brow. Thrushcross Grange was a prison and Edgar my gentle guard.

I was sitting at the window looking toward the rise of the hill, wishing I could leave my body behind and fly to the Heights. I wanted to be on the moor with Heathcliff, not as we were now but back when Father was alive and the two of us tumbled like puppies in the grass.

Nelly was pestering me, handing me something, telling me to read it. I had not the energy.

"It's a letter," Nelly said. "Shall I break the seal? Shall I read it to you? It's from Mr. Heathcliff."

The mention of his name brought me back to some sort of life. Nasty, prying, interfering Nelly! What would she do then? Go running to Edgar?

I've no idea what was in the letter. For then I heard Heathcliff's steps in the hall and there he was and I was in his arms. He was holding me so tight, kissing me so hard, I thought the two of us would merge into one.

"Cathy," Heathcliff said. "Oh, my life. How can I bear it?"

I leaned back so I could see his eyes. There was neither hope nor pity in them. Heathcliff knew I was dying, and he was in agony. I was filled with a sudden fury at the thought of leaving him. For he had done this. He was to blame.

"You have killed me, Heathcliff," I said. "You and Edgar have broken my heart between you. And now you both mourn and ask *me* to pity *your* suffering. But I shall give you none. You've killed me and thrived on it. How strong you are! How many years will you live after I am gone?"

Heathcliff tried to pull away, but I wound my fingers in his hair. I wanted to hurt him. "I wish I could hold you till we're both dead!" I cried. "I wouldn't care if you suffered. Why shouldn't you? I do. Will you be happy when I'm in the ground? Will you forget me? Will you say twenty years hence, 'That's the grave of Catherine Earnshaw. I loved her once and was sad to lose her, but I've loved others since. My children are dearer to me than she was.' At your death will you rejoice to come to me or will you be sorry to leave them?"

"Don't torture me till I'm as mad as you are," Heathcliff said, jerking his head out of my grasp and moving away. He swallowed my anger and spat it back out. "Are you possessed to talk like this while you're dying? Consider that those words will burn themselves into my memory, eating deeper for eternity! You lie to say I killed you, Cathy, and you know I could not forget you as much as I could forget my own existence. Is it not sufficient for your damned selfishness that while you shall be at peace I shall writhe in Hell?"

"I shall not be at peace!" I cried. "I'm not wishing you more torment than I have. I only wish us never to be parted. If a word of mine distresses you, I shall feel that same distress underground. Come back here. You never harmed me in my life. Don't be angry, not now. That will be worse for you to remember than my foolish words. Come back!"

But he would not. Heathcliff walked to the fireplace and stood raging with his back to me. And my mind slipped and I had the strangest feeling that it was not Heathcliff who stood there but an imposter.

"That is not my Heathcliff," I told Nelly. "I shall love mine and take him with me—he's in my soul. I shall escape this prison and fly into the glory of the world. I will see it clearly, not through tears, and I shall feel it fresh and bright, not with an aching heart."

The man at the fireplace turned and it was Heathcliff after all, his eyes wide and wet, his chest heaving with sobs. I so longed for him that I stood and tried to walk across the room.

I must have fallen, and Heathcliff must have caught me. For he was holding me. I tried to wipe away his tears, but they came too fast.

"How cruel you've been—cruel and false," Heathcliff said. "Why did you despise me? Why did you betray your own heart, Cathy? I cannot give you one word of comfort. You deserve this. You have killed yourself. You may kiss me and cry and wring out my kisses and tears and they will damn you to Hell. You loved me—what right had you to leave me? Why did you choose Edgar Linton? Nothing would have parted us—not misery or degradation or death—nothing that God or Satan could inflict. But you did it, of your own will. I have not broken your heart, you have broken mine. It is so much worse for me that I am strong. Do I want to live? What kind of living will it be when you . . . oh, God, I cannot think of it! Would you like to live with your soul in the grave?"

"Leave me alone," I said. "If I've done wrong, I'm dying for it. It is enough. You left me, but I won't scold you. I forgive you. Forgive me!"

"Oh, Cathy! I forgive what you have done to me. But how can I forgive what you've done to yourself! How can I?"

We were silent then. I buried my face in Heathcliff's shoulder. His face was against my neck. And we wept and wept at what we had come to.

And blasted Nelly Dean said, "Church service is over. Master will be back in half an hour."

We only held each other tighter. Time shrank and half an hour seemed to pass in a single breath.

"He is here!" Nelly fretted.

"I must go, Cathy," Heathcliff said. "But I'll see you again before you sleep. I won't stray five yards from your window."

"You must not go!" I said, for I could not bear it. "You shall not leave me again."

"Just for one hour."

"Not for a minute."

"I must," Heathcliff said. "Edgar will be up immediately."

But I clung to him fast. "No! Don't, don't go! It is the last time! Heathcliff, I shall die. I shall die!"

"Hush, my darling. Hush, hush, Cathy!" Heathcliff held me to his heart. "I'll stay," he said. "If Edgar shoots me, I'll die with your kisses on my lips."

Those words were the last I heard, and his kiss the last thing I felt.

17.

I have heard Nelly tell folk what happened next many times since, for the woman loves to gossip. By her account I fainted and Edgar was too concerned for me to care about what Heathcliff did or where he went.

At about midnight I delivered my daughter. Two hours later, without ever regaining consciousness, I slipped from the body that confined me. And I was right thinking I had no business to be in Heaven, for instead of rising up I stayed here on Earth.

So I saw Heathcliff standing as stiff as a piece of timber beneath the trees. Nelly slipped out to give him the news of my passing, and I heard her telling him I lay with a sweet smile on my face as if in a gentle dream. Nelly said she prayed I'd wake as sweetly in the other world.

And I heard my darling Heathcliff cursing me and wishing I might wake in the same torment as him. "She's a liar to the end!" he said. "Where is she? Not there . . . not in Heaven . . . not perished . . . where?"

"I am here," I said. But Heathcliff could not hear me.

"I pray one prayer," he told Nelly. "I will repeat it until my tongue is stiffened by death. Catherine Earnshaw, may you not rest as long as I am living. You said I killed you—haunt me then! Be with me always, take any form—drive me mad! Only do not leave me in this void where I cannot find you! Oh, God! It is unbearable. I cannot live without my life! I cannot live without my soul."

"I am here," I said again. "I am here."

But Heathcliff was dashing his head against the trunk of a tree, howling, so maddened with pain that I could not reach him.

*

I was put in the ground, buried not in the family crypt but at the place where churchyard meets moor. That night Heathcliff went to my grave and dug down to where my coffin lay with his own two hands. He thought to pull off the lid, to hold me in his arms once more.

I whispered, "Don't."

He still could not hear me, yet he sensed I was there.

That sense of me has tormented Heathcliff for twenty years. He'd walk into a room and feel that I'd just left. If he went out, he'd think he'd meet me on the moor. If he was on the moor, he thought I waited for him at home. Heathcliff turned his head, expecting to see me. But he never did. I was there all the time, standing right beside him, but he was so blinded by hate that he could not see.

Time passed. Events moved on. So many tragedies. So many deaths.

Poor, silly Isabella ran away from Heathcliff not long after I died. Their son was born the same month Hindley finally succeeded in drinking himself to death. My brother was so deeply in debt to Heathcliff by then that Wuthering Heights went not to Hareton, who should have been the rightful owner, but to Heathcliff.

Hareton grew up ignorant and uneducated. Heathcliff kept Hareton as an unpaid servant, who loved and blessed him for it, for Heathcliff had saved Hareton from his father.

Heathcliff's son grew up, as did my daughter. She had Edgar's fair skin and blonde hair, and looked more like Isabella than me. She was a loving, devoted darling, and exactly what Edgar deserved.

Heathcliff had never seen nor taken interest in his son, but when Isabella died, he took the boy back to Wuthering Heights. He was a weak, miserable little thing, unlikely to live long, and had the Linton looks. There was nothing of his father, Heathcliff, in him. But the boy was a useful weapon, and Heathcliff was devious enough to compel my daughter to marry his son. Edgar died from the sorrow of their marriage soon after. Heathcliff's son took the same fate a month later. My daughter was left an orphan and a widow, with her fate entirely in Heathcliff's hands.

Heathcliff now owned Thrushcross Grange as well as Wuthering Heights. It brought him no joy. His two great enemies, Hindley and Edgar, were dead and he had full possession of their property. But still he had no relief. The more he'd fed his desire for revenge, the greater it had grown. And Edgar's blood flowing in my daughter's veins and Hindley's blood in Hareton's only made it worse. Heathcliff was determined to crush them both too.

He would have done so. My daughter was a prisoner at the Heights, and Hareton Heathcliff's slave. Heathcliff would have reduced them both to beggary, and after that he'd have taken a pickaxe and smashed both houses to the ground, stone by stone. Yet still his vengeful appetite would not have been sated.

But then a passing stranger was caught out in a storm and forced to take shelter at Wuthering Heights. The stranger lay in my bed, he read my books, he spoke aloud the names I had scratched into the paint on the window ledge.

Catherine, Catherine, Catherine.

He repeated my name over and over again until the air swarmed with Catherines.

His incantation gave me form. The passing stranger saw the ghost of a child lost and wandering on the moor these last twenty years. That passing stranger gave Heathcliff proof of my continued existence.

It forced a crack in that great wall of Heathcliff's hatred, and I slipped through.

Perhaps it was only that. Or perhaps it was also that the two young people Heathcliff was bent on destroying began slowly but surely to fall in love. Despite him, and against all odds, Hareton and my daughter made a heaven out of hell.

Something different was in the air—a softness, a mutual joy. And it was so strong it began to seep into Heathcliff's bones and stir something in his heart.

Heathcliff took long walks on the moor. He visited all our places. He swam in the creek and lay in the long grass looking up at the sky. And one night he came home and saw Hareton and my daughter by the fire, heads close together, laughing. The sound carried Heathcliff back to a time when he and I laughed over something, nothing, anything. A time when we laughed until we were breathless and so weak we could hardly stand.

As they looked up at him, Heathcliff did not see Edgar in my daughter or Hindley in Hareton. He saw my eyes looking out from both their faces.

"Look at them, Heathcliff," I said. "They are how we could have been. How we should have been. How we could be still if you would only leave them be. Will you not come to me now, my love?"

And Heathcliff, my Heathcliff, turned.

He reached out his hand and said, "Cathy!"

Later, Nelly heard an upstairs window banging in the wind. When she went to close it, she found Heathcliff lying on his bed, soaked from the rain that had blown in during the night. He had a smile on his face so radiant that it was only when she touched his freezing skin that Nelly realized he was dead.

*

Hareton was the only living soul who truly grieved for Heathcliff. He married my daughter. The newlyweds moved to Thrushcross Grange, and Wuthering Heights was left to its ghosts.

Heathcliff and I walk the moor while my books crumble to dust. We watch from the cliff while the names on the window ledge wear away to nothing.

Catherine Earnshaw—the girl I was born.

Catherine Linton—the wife I became.

Catherine Heathcliff—who I am in my heart. Who I am in my soul.

We were then. Are now. And ever shall be.

Catherine. Heathcliff.

Our books are tested
for children and young people by
children and young people.

Thanks to everyone who consulted on
a manuscript for their time and effort in
helping us to make our books better
for our readers.